Hi, I'm Carrie  And David

Welcome to our **JUMP UP** and **JOIN IN** series.

We hope you enjoy reading the books and joining in with the songs.

This book is called **Meerkat's Mohican**.

This one really rocks and it's all about **confidence**.

It certainly is, remember to **turn the page** when you hear this sound . . .

TWANG!

EGMONT

We bring stories to life

First published in Great Britain 2013
by Egmont UK Limited,
The Yellow Building, 1 Nicholas Road, London W11 4AN
www.egmont.co.uk

Text copyright © Carrie and David Grant 2013
Illustrations copyright © Ailie Busby 2013

Carrie and David Grant and Ailie Busby have asserted their moral rights.

ISBN 978 1 4052 5835 7

A CIP catalogue record for this title is available from the British Library.

Please note:
Adult supervision is
recommended when
scissors are in use.

To our beautiful
children who
captivate us with
their music and
confidence.
– Carrie and David –

For Hamish x
– Ailie –

Carrie and David Grant

Meerkat's Mohican

Illustrations by Ailie Busby

Remember to turn the page when Meerkat's guitar **twangs!**

EGMONT

Bang! Bang!

Meerkat wanted to join the school rock band more than anything in the world.

"Practice makes perfect," said Meerkat, getting out his guitar.

But the music he made sounded more like Rock-a-Bye-Baby

than ROCK-AND-ROLL!

Soon his parents
were snoozing . . .

. . . and snoring!

"I'll NEVER be a ROCK STAR!" said Meerkat to Mr Maestro, his music teacher.

"Nonsense!" said Mr Maestro.
"You just need to *feel* the music.
Play along with me and you'll see."

Meerkat played his guitar along with
Mr Maestro's violin.

The music they made was very soothing but it still sounded more like a lullaby than a ROCK song.

When Meerkat got home from school
he told his mum how disappointing
his day had been.

"Little Meery-Mo, it sounds like you need a change," said Mum sympathetically. "Tomorrow we'll go to the hairdressers."

HARRIET HARE'S HAIR SALON

Meerkat had never been to the hairdressers.
He wasn't sure it would help his musical problem,
but he decided to give it a go.

His hair was washed and brushed

and combed and cut

and blow-dried

and gelled and coiffed

until Meerkat looked like . . .

A ROCK STAR!

That night he practised harder than ever.

"Now I look like a real *ROCK STAR*," he said,
"maybe I can play like one, too!"

The next day Meerkat auditioned for his school band . . .

Toot! Toot!

. . . and he totally ROCKED!

No one fell asleep this time – they were too busy dancing!

Meerkat knew that it wasn't his mohican but his CONFIDENCE that got the crowd rocking.

"Let's roll!" said Meerkat.

"You *ROCK*!" said his friends.

"Rock on!"

Everybody's rockin'
We all gotta dream.
Everybody's rockin'
Why don't you just scream?
Everybody's rockin'
We all gotta dream.
Everybody's rockin'
Why don't you just scream?

Yeah!
We gotta rock.
Gotta rock, gotta rock, gotta gotta rock.
Yeah!
We gotta rock.
Gotta rock, gotta rock, yeah,
    we gotta rock.

Chorus:
Everybody's rockin'
We all gotta dream.
Everybody's rockin'
Why don't you just scream?
Everybody's rockin'
We all gotta dream.
Everybody's rockin'
Why don't you just scream?

Yeah!
We gotta rock.
Gotta rock, gotta rock, gotta gotta rock.
Yeah!
We gotta rock.
Gotta rock, gotta rock, yeah,
    we gotta rock.

Jump, jump, jump, jump, jump, jump, jump.
Jump, jump, jump, jump, jump, jump.
Everybody . . .
Jump, jump, jump, jump, jump, jump, jump.
Jump, jump, jump, jump, jump, jump.

Ladies and Gentlemen!
Introducing on guitar . . .
Meerkat!

Now scream!
Let's go!

Chorus:
Everybody's rockin'
We all gotta dream.
Everybody's rockin'
Why don't you just scream?
Everybody's rockin'
We all gotta dream.
Everybody's rockin'
Why don't you just scream?

Yeah!
We gotta rock.
Gotta rock, gotta rock, gotta gotta rock.
Yeah!
We gotta rock.
Gotta rock, gotta rock, yeah,
    we gotta rock.

Jump, jump, jump, jump, jump, jump, jump.
Jump, jump, jump, jump, jump, jump.
Everybody . . .
Jump, jump, jump, jump, jump, jump, jump.
Jump, jump, jump, jump, jump, jump.

When you play Track **7**, the karaoke track, sing along
to the whole song! Your special solo parts are in **bold**.

Strike a Pose!

We hope you enjoyed the story.
This story was all about **confidence**.

 **Confidence** is a big part of singing and playing music.

Stand in front of a mirror and tell yourself, **"I look good!"** Keep your head up, put your shoulders back and **smile!**

You're looking good!

Now strike a really **cool** pose.

Oh yeah!

Next, stand with your feet apart and arms up and out in the air.

You really are a star! Just like Meerkat!

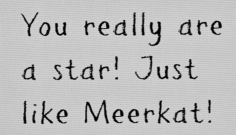

For our **Jump Up and Join In** series we really want to get children interested in music and how it works. It shouldn't be rocket science and we want to encourage you as a parent, teacher or carer to teach your children with confidence.
If **you** can learn it then **you** can pass it on.

Track 6 Pitch Perfect

In this book we're going to move on to **relative pitch.** This is the distance between one note and another. Let's start singing with the fingers on our hands counting up to eight, like this . . .

1
Lowest

2

3

4

5

6

7

8
Highest

Now we're going to count from one up to three, then straight back to one, then jump to three, then back to one.

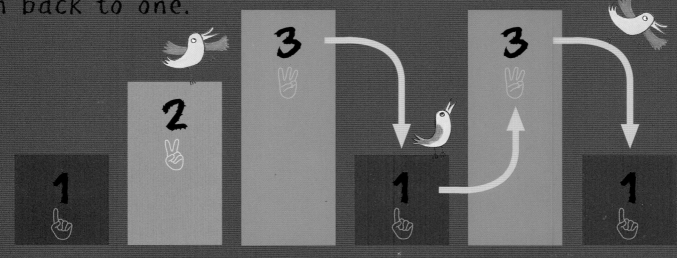

Now let's see if we can do it to four.

Now sing those two parts one after the other. If you manage that, then you're ready to move on to all eight . . .

Make your own
Shoebox Guitar!

Ask a grown-up to help you!

You'll need:

Shoebox   Cardboard tube (from kitchen roll)
Large rubber bands   Scissors   Straw   Glue

Step 1 Draw a saucer-sized circle on the shoebox lid and cut it out. Draw around the cardboard tube on one end of the shoebox and cut that out too.

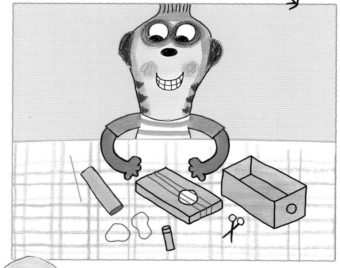

Step 2 Stretch the rubber bands around the lid (you can use two or three or four) and position them over the hole.

Step 4 Now go ahead and strum those strings!

Step 3 Put the lid back on the box and secure with two more elastic bands. Cut the straw in half and slide the two pieces under the rubber bands at each end of the guitar and glue in place. Slide the cardboard tube into the hole.

About Carrie and David

Carrie and David are best known for their hugely successful CBeebies series, **Carrie and David's Popshop**. They have coached Take That, The Saturdays and the Spice Girls and have a top-selling vocal coaching book and DVD. In 2008 they were awarded a BASCA for their lifetime services to the music industry.

Parents to four children, Carrie and David are passionate about getting all children to sing and are keen to encourage adults to feel more confident in teaching their little ones music skills from an early age. The **Jump Up And Join In** series was born as a result of this passion and will help young children learn a set of basic skills and develop a real love of music. As ambassadors for **Sing Up** – a not-for-profit organisation providing the complete singing solution for schools – and judges of the young singers on BBC 1's **Comic Relief Does Glee Club**, Carrie and David believe children everywhere should be given the tools to enjoy, and to feel confident about, practising music in all its shapes and forms.

Thanks for jumping up
and joining in!
Till the next time, bye!